Disney Bambi

This is the story of a fawn who grew up
to be the Great Prince of the Forest.

Printed in the U.S.A • ISBN: 1-61524-327-5

Disney Handle Box Set Book - Bambi • 10 11 12 13 B&M 35652 10 9 8 7 6 5 4 3 2

One spring morning, there was great excitement in the
forest. Animals and birds hurried to welcome the new
Prince. His name was Bambi. He was the son of a noble
stag, the Great Prince of the Forest.

When Bambi looked around, he saw happy, smiling faces.
"They call me Thumper," said a friendly rabbit.
Bambi smiled.

It wasn't long before Bambi was ready to explore the forest with his best friend, Thumper. Birds sang and fluttered over their heads. Thumper pointed at them and said, "Those are birds."

Bambi repeated the word. "Bir-duh!"

Then a butterfly fluttered by. Bambi called out, "Bird!"

"No," said Thumper with a giggle. "That's a butterfly."

Bambi turned to a pretty flower and shouted, "Butterfly!"

Thumper laughed. "No!" he cried. "That's a flower!"

Bambi bent down to smell the flowers. Suddenly, a small black-and-white head popped up from under the petals.

"Flower!" said Bambi again. Thumper laughed, "That's not a flower. He's a little…"

"That's all right," the little skunk said shyly. "He can call me a flower if he wants to."

They all became good friends.

One morning, Bambi's mother took him to a new place—the wide, open meadow.

"You must never rush out," said Bambi's mother. "There are no trees or bushes to hide us."

Bambi met another fawn. Her name was Faline. Bambi and Faline became friends, too.

Just then, a group of stags charged across the meadow, led by the Great Prince. He had come to warn the deer that there was danger nearby, and to run toward the trees.

Later that day, Bambi asked his mother what the danger had been.

"Man was in the forest," she told him.

Summer and autumn passed, and the weather grew colder. One morning, Bambi woke up to find that the world had turned white! Bambi's mother saw his surprise.

"It's snow," she said. "Winter has come."

Bambi was amazed to find his friend Thumper sliding across an icy pond.

"Come on—it's all right!" called Thumper. "Look! The water's stiff!"

Bambi rushed over to join him—but he fell down onto his tummy with a *thud!*

Thumper showed Bambi how to balance on the ice. Soon the young Prince was gliding gracefully across the pond, too.

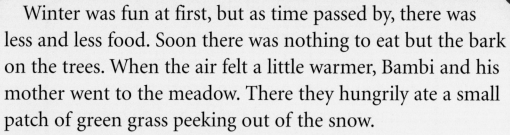

Winter was fun at first, but as time passed by, there was less and less food. Soon there was nothing to eat but the bark on the trees. When the air felt a little warmer, Bambi and his mother went to the meadow. There they hungrily ate a small patch of green grass peeking out of the snow.

Suddenly, Bambi's mother looked up and sniffed the air. "Quick!—the thicket!" she ordered Bambi. "Faster!"

Bambi raced across the meadow. Then there was a loud *bang*!

"Faster, Bambi. Don't look back!" his mother shouted.

As he ran, there was another loud *bang*! Terrified, Bambi kept running toward the forest. Home at last, Bambi turned to look for his mother.

"Mother! Where are you?" he called. There was no answer. "Mother! Mother!"

The little fawn began to cry.

Just then, Bambi's father appeared by his side.

"Your mother can't be with you anymore," he told Bambi gently.

The Great Prince would now protect his son until he could look after himself.

As the months passed, Bambi grew into a fine young stag.

One sunny, spring day, all the birds were twittering and snuggling.

"Hmph!" said Friend Owl to Bambi and Thumper. "They're twitterpated! Nearly everybody gets twitterpated in the springtime."

"It's not going to happen to me!" Thumper said.

"Me neither," Bambi agreed.

Minutes later, a lovely female rabbit hopped over to Thumper. He was delighted.

"Twitterpated," sighed Bambi, as he went on alone through the trees.

Bambi stopped to drink at a small pond. A soft voice said, "Hello, Bambi." He turned around and saw a beautiful female deer. It was Faline, his childhood friend.

Faline leaned over and gently licked Bambi's face. And he became twitterpated, too!

The warm days of spring and summer passed happily for Bambi and Faline.

Early one autumn morning, Bambi was awakened by a strange smell. He left Faline sleeping in the forest and went to investigate.

Bambi climbed to the top of a cliff. He could see smoke in the distance.

Just then, his father came up beside him.

"It is Man," said the Great Prince. "He is here again. We must go deep into the forest—hurry!"

Bambi rushed back to warn Faline. He found her trapped on a cliff ledge. A pack of angry hunting dogs was snapping at her heels!

As Bambi rushed at the snarling dogs, Faline managed to escape, and she ran toward the river.

Bambi fought off the dogs and turned to follow Faline. Suddenly, he heard a loud *bang*! He felt a terrible pain in his shoulder and fell to the ground.

Bambi was too weak to move, though he saw flames coming toward him. The forest was on fire!

"Get up, Bambi!" a voice called out. "You must get up! Come with me!"

Bambi opened his eyes and saw his father beside him. The young Prince struggled to his feet and followed his father through the burning forest.

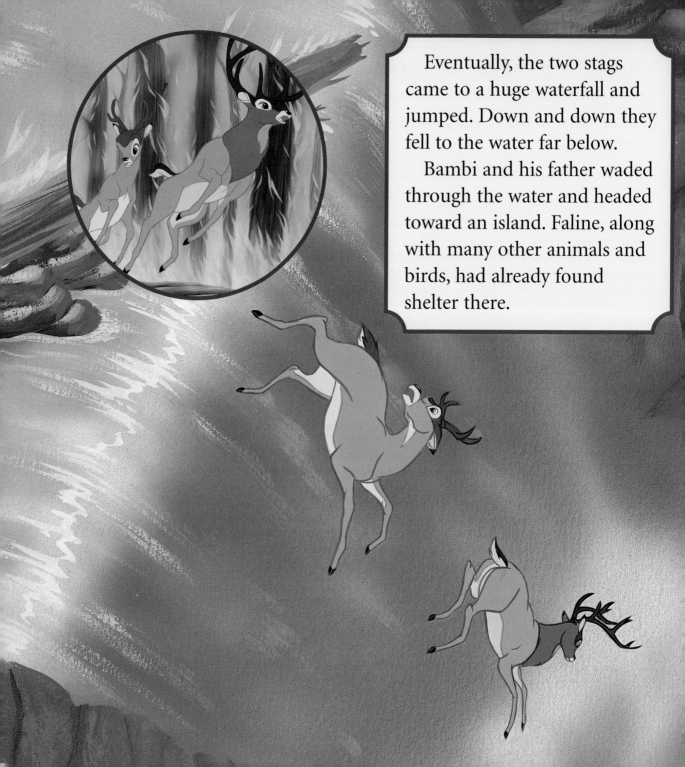

Eventually, the two stags came to a huge waterfall and jumped. Down and down they fell to the water far below.

Bambi and his father waded through the water and headed toward an island. Faline, along with many other animals and birds, had already found shelter there.

Safe on the island, the forest creatures watched helplessly as the fire destroyed their homes. Then, when the fire finally burned out, the animals returned to the forest.

After another long, hard winter, spring arrived. New grass and flowers grew where the fire had been. The forest was beautiful once again.

One warm morning, Thumper and Flower spread some wonderful news. Bambi and Faline had a family.

All the animals and birds came to see Faline and her two new fawns.

Standing nearby was their proud father,
Bambi, the new Great Prince of the Forest.